THE SMALLEST STEGOSAURUS

BY LYNN SWEAT AND LOUIS PHILLIPS · ILLUSTRATED BY LYNN SWEAT

Puffin Books

For Cathy and Ricki
—L.S.

For Amy and Nancy of Lab School fame
—L.P.

This text has been read for scientific accuracy by Dr. Peter Dodson, University of Pennsylvania.
The art was prepared in pencil on two-ply Scrathmore kid finish. The drawings were then fixed and
a thin wash of oils was laid over in the manner of a watercolor.

PUFFIN BOOKS
Published by the Penguin Group
Penguin Books USA Inc., 375 Hudson Street, New York, New York 10014, U.S.A.
Penguin Books Ltd, 27 Wrights Lane, London W8 5TZ, England
Penguin Books Australia Ltd, Ringwood, Victoria, Australia
Penguin Books Canada Ltd, 10 Alcorn Avenue, Toronto, Ontario, Canada M4V 3B2
Penguin Books (N.Z.) Ltd, 182-190 Wairau Road, Auckland 10, New Zealand

Penguin Books Ltd, Registered Offices: Harmondsworth, Middlesex, England

First published in the United States of America by Viking Penguin,
a division of Penguin Books USA Inc., 1993
Published in Puffin Books, 1995

3 5 7 9 10 8 6 4 2

Text copyright © Lynn Sweat and Louis Phillips, 1993
Illustrations copyright © Lynn Sweat, 1993
All rights reserved

THE LIBRARY OF CONGRESS HAS CATALOGED THE VIKING PENGUIN EDITION AS FOLLOWS:
Sweat, Lynn.
The smallest stegosaurus / by Lynn Sweat and Louis Phillips; illustrations by Lynn Sweat.   p.   cm.
Summary: Although he is small, a baby Stegosaurus wants to find a way to help his family like the other big, strong dinosaurs.
ISBN 0-670-83865-9
[1. Dinosaurs—Fiction. 2. Size—Fiction.] I. Phillips, Louis. II. Title.
PZ7.S9742Sm   1993   [E]—dc20   91-47730   CIP   AC

Puffin Books ISBN 0-14-054389-9

Printed in the United States of America

Dawn.

It was the dawn of a new day 150 million years ago.

There were no butterflies or flowers.

There were no cats or dogs. There were no people then.

But the sun rose red and warm over a large swamp,
and the air hummed with dragonflies. And spiders.

4

In this swamp, as the sun began to warm the air,

a family–a Stegosaurus family–awoke.

The mother and father Stegosaurus
were nearly twenty feet long.

Unfortunately, the smallest Stegosaurus was only
a few feet long. He had not yet grown armour.
He felt quite helpless in the big world.

He wanted to be big and strong.
He wanted to protect his parents from
their enemies–the dreadful Allosaurus
and the terrifying Ceratosaurus.

No matter which way the smallest Stegosaurus turned,
the world looked very large. Very large indeed.

Down by the ocean, he watched strange fish.
He wished he could swim like them.
If he could swim, he would feel safe underwater.

The smallest Stegosaurus looked
into the water and saw the shadows of
huge Pterodactyls flying overhead.

The smallest Stegosaurus suddenly became very
frightened. He ran toward the shade of a giant fern.
Because he was so tiny, he was able to hide easily.

He certainly didn't want to be picked up
in the sharp claws of the Pterodactyls
and carried high over the smoking volcanoes.

The smallest Stegosaurus was having his lunch
of leaves and twigs. He looked up just in time
to see a great foot coming toward him.

The foot belonged to an Allosaurus!

The giant foot nearly flattened the little Stegosaurus into the ground. The Stegosaurus rolled away just in time.

The smallest Stegosaurus ran deeper
into the forest to look for his parents.

He found them guarding a large egg
which they had buried in the sand.

When the smallest Stegosaurus told his father and mother
about his adventure with the Allosaurus,
they brought him into the comfort and safety of the large nest.

They taught him how to guard the egg
so that no Ornitholestes would steal it.

Ornitholestes were dinosaurs that were so fast they could catch flying birds. Their name, in fact, means "bird robber."

But they also liked to eat the eggs of other dinosaurs.

The smallest Stegosaurus kept a sharp lookout
for these robbers. He saw one by the lake.
His parents did not see it.

The smallest Stegosaurus cried out a warning, so his parents would be ready to tear the thief apart with their sharp tail spikes. The Ornitholestes ran into the swamp. The smallest Stegosaurus felt very proud that he was able to help his parents.

And then one day the egg hatched.
The shell cracked open, and out came
a brand new Stegosaurus—a tiny Stegosaurus.

The Stegosaurus now had a baby sister
who was much smaller than he was.

And, best of all, there was a whole new world to show her— a world of smoking volcanoes, giant ferns, inland seas, gigantic trees, stars, oceans. All this to share with her.

The no-longer-smallest Stegosaurus
suddenly felt very big. Very big indeed.

And all this happened in a time before
there were butterflies or flowers.
Before there were cats and dogs.

Before there were people.
When there were dinosaurs.

Stegosaurus (steg-uh-SAWR-us) means "plated lizard." These dinosaurs were so named because of the two rows of large bony plates that were arranged along their backs. The plates made the *Stegosaurus* (which usually measured between 20 and 30 feet long, and about 11 feet tall at the hips) appear larger, hence more frightening to its enemies. Some contemporary scientists speculate, however, that the plates were used to control the *Stegosaurus*'s body temperature. Wind flowed around the plates and cooled the *Stegosaurus*'s blood.

Stegosaurs, which roamed North America some 150 million years ago, were plant-eaters, not flesh-eaters, and they were probably neither very aggressive nor very smart. Although the adult *Stegosaurus*, with back legs more than twice as long as its front ones, was as big as an Asian elephant, its brain weighed less than two ounces and was no bigger than a walnut or a golf ball.

Four long spikes at the end of its tail, approximately one hundred very sharp teeth, and the pointed plates along its back were probably its best defense against "the dreadful Allosaurus and the terrifying Ceratosaurus." Using its ten-foot-long tail, the *Stegosaurus* could whip the spikes over its head and deep into an enemy's flesh.

L.P.